The Adventures of PHANTOM and PINKY

Dremon

Copyright © 2019 Dremon
All rights reserved
Second Edition

DREMONARC ENTERPRISES
PUBLISHING
Clarendon Terrace
Frederick, MD 21703

ISBN 978-1-7371285-0-2 (Paperback)
ISBN 978-1-7371285-1-9 (Digital)

Printed in the United States of America

For Addison and Caitlyn, my Phantom and Pinky

Grumpy Ol' Kitty

In a quiet little neighborhood lived a grumpy old kitty by the name of Phantom. Phantom spent his days lying around the house, being very sad and very grumpy, but he was not always that way.

He remembered the days he and his brother chased each other around their house, playing all sorts of kitty games. But those days were no more. His brother Casper was gone, living a separate life with a separate family. This made Phantom sad and the sadness became loneliness, and the loneliness became grumpiness. Phantom's owners, Mr. and Mrs. C, saw this and decided to get a new friend for Phantom, someone he can play with, run with, and jump with again.

The day finally arrived when Phantom was to get a new friend, but Phantom was grumpy with the whole idea of a new friend. "I don't want a new friend" said Phantom. "They will never be like my brother Casper" he thought. So he remained grumpy. In fact, when Mr. C brought home the new friend, Phantom ran away.

Grumpy Ol' Kitty

"Phantom, here is your new friend, Pinky. Please come and say hi," Mr. C exclaimed, but Phantom refused to come out. Mr. and Mrs. C told Phantom, "Sometimes it is hard to meet new people, but you will never know how great a friend can be until you first introduce yourself to them."

Mrs. C once read a book that cats are better introduced by keeping each cat in a separate room and letting them play under the door separating the rooms. She suggested that they give it a try.

Grumpy Ol' Kitty

Mr. C thought, "Well, nothing else is working. Let's give it a shot."

Pinky was a little fellow; very friendly, and full of energy, so naturally, he jumped at any chance to play. He stuck his paw under the door with a little encouragement from Mr. C, who had Phantom on the other side of the door. When Phantom saw this, he leapt from Mr. C's lap and jammed his paw under the door to play with Pinky on the other side.

Slowly they began to play with each other, then they played with each other with no doors between them, then eventually, they became great friends. Phantom was not grumpy anymore or sad, and he found a great friend in Pinky. That goes to show, great friends always start out as someone new, but if you give them a chance, they may become your best friends, like Phantom and Pinky.

The End

Lost in the Storm

It was another beautiful day in Barwood City. Phantom and Pinky were outside enjoying the cool breeze. What Phantom and Pinky did not know is the beautiful weather was about to change. For, you see, there was a bad storm coming their way.

It wasn't too long before dark clouds blocked the beautiful clear skies.

Pinky wondered, "Oh no! Where is the sun?"

Phantom replied, "I don't know, Pinky, but we should get back home soon."

They both started to run as fast as they could. *Clash*! *bang* went the lightning and thunder.

"Phantom, I am scared," said Pinky as they raced home.

Phantom said, "Don't worry. When we get home, everything will be okay."

Lost in the Storm

They ran as fast through the woods as they could and, finally, made it home.

"See, we made it home everything will be fine now," said Phantom, as he looked behind for Pinky. But when he turned, there was no Pinky. He called out, "Pinkyyy," but got no answer. The two had gotten separated while running through the woods, but Phantom did not notice.

He started to run back toward the woods, when *blam, thud!* a tree was hit by lightning and fell on his path. Phantom thought it best to go inside and wait until the storm passed.

Phantom looked outside as the storm raged on, hoping to see Pinky emerge from the shadows, but there was no Pinky. Phantom was worried. The storm finally passed, and Phantom raced out to the woods.

"What a mess," he thought. There were leaves and branches everywhere, but no sign of Pinky. He looked and looked. He called and called, but no Pinky.

Lost in the Storm

It was getting late and Phantom had to go back home. He promised he would keep looking every day until he could find Pinky. Two days passed with no luck, but at the end of the third day, as Phantom started to head back home after a long day of searching, he heard a faint rustle in the bushes. And then up popped a little black-and-white head.

It was Pinky! Hooray! Phantom raced over and hugged Pinky.

"Phantom, you were right. I was not scared and everything was okay. I hid in a hollow log until the storm passed, but then I couldn't find my way back home."

"Never mind now," said Phantom. "The important thing is you are safe."

"Let's go home."

And home they went, the two friends have found each other once again.

The End

The Mud Jump Contest

Phantom and Pinky was up to their old tricks.

"I bet you can't catch me," said Pinky, and off he dashed.

Phantom said, "Oh yeah," and off he went after him.

Pinky ran up big hill, he ran around frog pond, he ran down to Sheppard's meadow, and he ran through the small forest behind their home. Pinky was fast, but in the end, Phantom finally caught him just before he got to the bridge at Fisher creek.

"See, I told I would catch you," Phantom boasted.

"Yeah? Well, I was getting tired anyway," stated Pinky. Pinky was a bit competitive at times, so he didn't like that Phantom was boasting. "It is not nice to boast," Pinky said. "Well, I know another game you can't beat me at."

The Mud Jump Contest

"What game is that?" asked Phantom.

Pinky did not know what to say, so he just said, "You will find out tomorrow."

As the two friends walked back home, only Phantom did the talking. Pinky was off in his own head, trying to think of a game which he could beat Phantom at. He thought and thought until they both reached home. He thought about it during dinner time, he thought about it during bath time, he thought about it while brushing his teeth, and he even thought about it when he was in bed. The only time he stopped thinking about it was when he heard a loud crack outside and then the rain began to fall.

"That's it," Pinky thought. "After the rain, there will be lots mud puddles. We can see who is the best at jumping mud puddles."

The next day came, and Pinky was very excited to play puddle jump with Phantom. He thought, "For sure, I will beat him at this game. After all, Phantom is older than I am and he is not as nimble as I am, so I should beat him very easily."

Pinky told Phantom about the new game he wants to play, and Phantom was very excited to try this new game. Phantom was very glad to play for the fun of the game, but all Pinky could think about was the competition. He wanted nothing more than to beat Phantom once and for all.

The game began, and over the first puddle went Pinky with ease. Phantom followed shortly and also cleared the first puddle with ease. "Okay, that was an easy one," said Pinky. "Now let's try something a bit harder."

The Mud Jump Contest

Pinky looked for a bigger puddle to jump over. *Zwoooop*! over he went with not much effort, and again, Phantom did the same. Pinky started to look a bit frustrated, and looked for an even bigger puddle to jump over.

The game kept on the same way. Every puddle Pinky jumped, Phantom jumped as well. Finally, Pinky got so upset and he looked for the biggest puddle he could find. It took Pinky a while to find it, but there it was, right on the edge of the great pond, a puddle so big they both gulped when they saw it.

They thought it was just like the other puddles they jumped over before, but what they didn't know was that it rained so hard in the night that it created a large hole at the edge of the great pond, a very deep, very long hole filled with water and thick mud like quicksand. To Phantom and Pinky, it may have looked like a very big puddle, but it was much more dangerous than they could imagine.

The Mud Jump Contest

"I am not so sure about this, Pinky," said Phantom. "Let's just stop now and go home."

"Don't be such a fraidy cat," replied Pinky. "Last one over is a rotten egg," Pinky shouted, knowing for sure this time he was going to beat Phantom.

Pinky made a running start, and then *whooooosh*, through the air he went and barely made it to the other side of the puddle. Now Phantom didn't feel so afraid because he thought if Pinky can do it so can I.

Phantom backed up and made a running start toward the puddle, then off he went—up, up, up then down, down, down. Oh no! *Splash*! Phantom fell into the puddle and started to sink.

"HELP! HELP!" he shouted. "Pinky, I can't get out. The more I move the more I sink."

Pinky was very shocked and didn't know what to do. "I am so sorry, Phantom. It's is all my fault," Pinky said over and over again.

The Mud Jump Contest

"It's okay, Pinky," said Phantom. "Please just help me."

Luckily, Pinky noticed a piece of branch that broke off one of trees during the night. He dragged it over to the puddle and pushed it down the side of the puddle.

Phantom's feet touched the branch, and he was able to climb out of the muddy puddle to safety.

"I will never let my pride get in the way again Phantom," said Pinky.

Phantom replied, "It's not just your fault, Pinky. I will never try something that is beyond my abilities. I also let pride get in the way of good sense."

"Let's go home," said Pinky, and the two friends went home with a sigh of relief and a lesson learned: to never let pride cause them to do things that they know are not right.

The End

Hanging by a Thread

Phantom and Pinky was at it again, playing their usual games. This time their games took them to the top of Shelby Hill. Shelby Hill was a very dangerous hill. There were many accidents on Shelby Hill.

Phantom tried to warn Pinky not to play too close to the edge. Pinky did not listen. "Hey, Phantom, watch me," he said.

Pinky made a huge leap in the air from a small boulder to an even bigger boulder. When he landed on the boulder, he lost his footing and slipped down the boulder and then down the side of Shelby Hill. Luckily, there was a branch there to catch his fall.

"Pinky," shouted Phantom with a very worried look on his face.

Phantom very carefully looked over the side of the hill. He was relieved to find Pinky hanging on to the tiny branch.

"Help me," said Pinky.

"Hold on, Pinky," Phantom said, and he rushed off to find something to pull up Pinky.

He ran to the nearest tree looking for anything that could help. He found an old bicycle tire. Can this can help Pinky? *No*! So he kept looking.

He found a baseball bat. Can this help Pinky? *No*! So he kept looking.

Then he found a long vine on the tree next to the nearest tree. Can this help Pinky? *Yes*! Yes, it can.

Just then Phantom had a great idea. "I will tie one end of the vine to the old bicycle tire, then I will tie the other end to this old baseball bat," said Phantom. "Then I will lower the bicycle tire to Pinky, wrap the baseball bat around the nearest tree, and use the baseball bat as a handle around the tree to pull up Pinky."

Phantom followed his plan, and it worked. Pinky was once again safe and sound back at the top of Shelby Hill.

Pinky gave Phantom a great big hug and said, "Let's go home, Phantom. I never want to see this hill again."

Phantom told Pinky to not to be afraid of Shelby Hill. He told him, "When we have bad experiences in life, we cannot give up and say we don't want to do it anymore. You had a bad experience at Shelby Hill. Don't give up and say you are not going back. Be more careful and think about what you can do to have fun in a safe way."

Pinky agreed with Phantom, and the two friends returned to the safety of their home.

The End

Meowmy's Last Day

Summer had come and gone, and it was time for everyone to go back to school. Everyone visiting Barrwood City was going back to their homes. One of the visitors leaving was Pinky's newest friend, Meowmy.

Meowmy was from Japan and came to visit her aunt in Barrwood City. It was a sad day. Pinky did not want to say good-bye to his new friend. "It's not fair," said Pinky. "I still have many more games I want to play with you."

Pinky was upset. He was not being nice to Meowmy. Meowmy tried to say good-bye, but Pinky just turned his back to her and then ran away.

Phantom saw how Pinky behaved and chased after him. When Phantom found Pinky, he asked why he ran away from their friend, Meowmy. Pinky started sobbing and told Phantom that Meowmy was leaving them.

Pinky said, "I don't want to be friends with her anymore."

Phantom told Pinky, "Just because your friend has to leave, does not mean you should be mean to your friends."

Just then wise, old Phantom reminded Pinky that sometimes, whether we like it or not, people have to leave.

"Some people may leave after a long time being with you, and others may leave after a short time," Phantom said. "Sometimes the best thing we can do is remember the time we spend with them. Keep those memories with you always, so even if they have to leave, they will always be with you."

Pinky stopped sobbing. He looked at Phantom and said, "You are right, Phantom," with the biggest smile on his face. "I have to tell Meowmy that I am sorry."

Pinky raced to find Meowmy. "Meeeooooowmy! Meeeooooowmy!" he shouted when he spotted her getting into the taxi. "Don't leave. I have to tell you something!"

Meowmy stopped and got out of the taxi. Pinky finally caught up to her.

"I am so sorry, Meowmy. I should not have been mean to you. I am glad we became friends, and I did not want you to leave without apologizing. I promise I will write to you, and we can see each other on the computer."

"I would like that very much, Pinky," Meowmy said.

The two friends hugged each other, and Meowmy got in the taxi and drove away. Pinky ran behind the taxi, waving at Meowmy, shouting, "Bye, Meowmy! See you again soon."

Meowmy's Last Day

Pinky waved until he could no longer see Meowmy and the taxi.

Pinky was not sad because he remembered what Phantom said and remembered all his memories of the fun Meowmy and he had throughout the summer.

The End

Friendship Day Picnic

It was a very hot and humid summer in Barwood City. Phantom and Pinky came up with a great idea to beat the heat.

"We can do a picnic on the banks of Princess Creek under the old oak tree," said Phantom.

"We can invite all of our friends," said Pinky.

"We will call it Friendship Day Picnic," said Phantom.

So they called Meowmy, Sugary, Brown Sugar, Butterscotch, and Chocolate Chip. Their other friend Cotton Ball was out of town, but all the friends they called said yes. They will come.

Everyone started to make preparations for the picnic. Butterscotch said she will bring a cake, Chocolate Chip and Brown Sugar was going to bring games, Sugary and Meowmy said they will both bring water and fruit juices, and Phantom and Pinky said they will bring sandwiches and chips for everyone.

"This is going to be the best day ever," said Pinky. We get to eat and have fun with all of our friends. Only Cotton Ball is missing. I wish Cotton Ball was here."

The night before Friendship Day Picnic everyone was busy making preparations. They were all so excited they could hardly contain themselves. Everyone completed their tasks one by one.

Pinky and Phantom were done with all the sandwiches, and the chips were all in a bag ready to go. Butterscotch made a beautiful cake and sat it out on her table to cool overnight, and Sugary and Meowmy bought all the juices and water for everyone. Brown Sugar and Chocolate Chip went in

Friendship Day Picnic

their closets and pulled out all the games they could find. They made two bundles of games one for each to carry.

Early the next morning, everyone left on their way to the picnic. Each one of the friends had a different route to the picnic. They all had short walks, but some areas were more dangerous than others.

Phantom and Pinky had to walk over the bridge at Chomper's pond, named for the fishes that live in the pond. They have very big, sharp teeth and love to chomp. Pinky and Phantom had to be very careful when they cross over the bridge.

Friendship Day Picnic

Slowly and steadily, they crossed the thin but sturdy bridge. The food rocked back and forth on Phantom and Pinky's backs as they crossed, but they made it across.

Soon thereafter, they all met up under the old oak tree, just at the mouth of Princess Creek. It was all decorated with a great big banner that had words written on it, "Welcome to the First Annual Friendship Day Picnic."

Everything looked so beautiful. Soon everyone was having a great time playing games and enjoying the food and drinks. It was all going so well, then the fun stopped, and everyone looked to the sky.

There they saw something falling from the sky, and everyone started to wonder what it was. "What is this strange object falling from the sky?" As the object got closer, it started to take the shape of someone and not something.

Butterscotch shouted, "LOOK! IT'S COTTON BALL."

And sure enough, it was Cotton Ball. He came to surprise them. He heard about the picnic from Pinky when they spoke over the phone and decided it was not a picnic that he could miss.

Cotton Ball made a grand entrance by landing with his parachute just at the edge of Princess Creek, which was a close call because he nearly landed in the creek. Everyone was overjoyed to see Cotton Ball; he made it a day to remember.

Pinky jumped up on a low hanging branch of the old oak tree and said, "This will be the best Friendship Day Picnic ever!"

The End

Friendship Day Picnic

Day at the Zoo

It was a beautiful sunny day and a great day for the zoo. Phantom and Pinky piled into the car and off they went. Whoohooo!

It was a mad dash to get to the zoo; they even got lost on the way. It was a great adventure still, especially on this day.

They finally made it to the zoo and were so excited too. They could hardly contain themselves. They were happier than Santa's elves.

They parked and hurried to the ticket counter. "Two tickets please," said Phantom.

Pinky was so beside himself, he nearly had a tantrum.

Day at the Zoo

Soon they were on their way to see the animals, but not soon enough. For Pinky ran so fast, he tripped and nearly fell into some nasty stuff. Phantom told him to slow down, but he did not listen. Now he was crying for he had fallen and his favorite hat was miss'n.

Phantom came over and said to not worry. "We will find your favorite hat." He knew where it was and pointed aloft. "Do you see where it's at?"

They both looked over, and there on the head of a pelican was indeed where it sat.

"My hat! My hat!" said Pinky with glee. "We only have one problem. Who will fetch it for me?"

Just then, the pelican said, "No problem, my friend. I will bring it for you, if some time you will spend."

Pinky and Phantom did just that and made a new friend with a pelican named Pat.

Next they stopped to see the birds of prey, alligators, and panthers too. They were a sight to see, but there were more at the zoo. So they continued on and visited the coati, which was busy digging and searching for food. He looked up long enough just to say hi; for he remembered his mommy told him not to be rude.

Day at the Zoo

Their next stop was the white-tailed deer and, after that, the big, black bear. In fact, the bear was taking a nap; nothing could wake him, not even a snap.

Phantom and Pinky walked slowly through the zoo, observing every animal in their habitat. They did not want the day to end, as they moved from there to that.

The zoo was so amazing and was such a fascinating place. Then Phantom and Pinky hurried with a hasty pace. They were off to see the river otters; who will win the race?

They were delighted to see the otters swimming and were sad when they had to go, but there were still much to see, and the zoo still had so much to show. So on they went, giddy as can be; the bush dog, tapir, and

Day at the Zoo

jaguar they did see. They saw a giant anteater, a capybara, and a Patagonian cavy, animals they have never heard or seen before but were quite savvy. Then there were monkeys: spider, capuchin, goeldis, and black howlers. They saw New Guinea singing dogs, which were known as singers not growlers. They saw other cats, like tigers, servals, and ocelots. They tried to see them all, but could not because the zoo had lots. The golden lion tamarin, lemurs, and koalas were ever so cute, and they even saw wallabies and a kangaroo named Brute. They even saw the biggest bird ever. The enclosure was labelled "emu." They also saw the biggest lizards they have ever seen; there were two.

Finally, the day was over for Phantom and Pinky. As they passed the big cats again, they smelled something quite stinky. They hurried past the smell and to the final exhibit; there they saw the ghost of an alligator.

Day at the Zoo

Pinky asked, "What is it?"

It was a special alligator, as white as can be. Phantom declared, "I have never seen an alligator that is so easy to see," as it just lay there under the sun.

Pinky then urged, "Please move, Mr. Alligator. If you stay much longer, you will be well done."

Phantom told Pinky with a small grin, "Don't worry, Pinky. He has protection from his thick skin."

As they stared in amazement at their friend, the alligator, whose name they don't know, Phantom suddenly realized that it was time for them to

go. So out they went and back into the car to start their journey home, which was closer than far.

They both treasured the joy and knew what it meant, the great time they had, the little time they spent. They loved all the animals there on display, and will forever remember them as they drove home that day.

Do Not Share

"AAAGGGHHHH CHOOOOOOOO!"

"Pinky?" Phantom exclaimed, as he tried to catch all his papers that were now scattered everywhere. Pinky had the loudest sneeze he has ever heard, and it had blown all of Phantom's artwork all over the room.

"Pinky," said Phantom. "Don't you know to cover your nose when you sneeze?"

"I'mmm soooryyy," said Pinky. But no one ever taught me."

"I know how you can remember," said Phantom. "When you feel a sneeze coming on just remember, *do not share*."

"I was always taught to share," said Pinky, "and now you are telling me not to share."

Do Not Share

"No," said Phantom. "I am not telling you not to share. 'Do not share' is something that can help you remember what to do when you are going to sneeze. It mean

D	**O.**	**N**	**O**	**T**	**S**	**H**	**A**	**R**	**E**
I	*N*	*O*	*N*	*O*	*L*	*A*	*R*	*A*	*L*
P	*E*	*S*			*E*	*N*	*M*	*G*	*B*
'S	*E*				*E*	*D*			*O*
					V	*K*			*W*
					E	*E*			
						R			
						C			
						H			
						I			
						E			
						F			

Dip One's Nose onto Sleeve, Handkerchief, Arm, Rag, or Elbow."

"So what does this have to do with sharing?" asked Pinky.

Phantom replied, "There is one thing you should not share. Can you guess what it is? I know! Let's make it a game. If you can guess the right answer, I will buy you ice cream."

"Yeah!" said Pinky. "You have yourself a deal."

Do Not Share

Pinky: Is it my toys?
Phantom: No. You can share your toys.
Pinky: Is it my books?
Phantom: No. You can share your books.
Pinky: Is it my food?
Phantom: No. You can share your food.
Pinky: Is it my crayons?
Phantom: No. You can share your crayons.
Pinky: Is it my games?
Phantom: No. You can share your games.
Pinky: Is it my bike?
Phantom: No. You can share your bike
Pinky: Is it my teddy bear?
Phantom: No. You can share your teddy bear.
Pinky: Is it my juice?
Phantom: No. You can share your juice, but be careful because you can pass them on or pick them up.

Do Not Share

Pinky: I give up. I don't know what I should not share

Phantom: Don't give up, Pinky. I will give you a clue. When you wash your hands after touching dirty things, what don't you want to share?

Pinky: I don't want to share my soap?

Phantom: No. You can share your soap. It helps to get rid of them.

Pinky: Oh, I know. I wash my hands to get rid of them. Is it germs?

Phantom: Yes yes. You got it! That is why I taught you the motto, 'Do not share.' Because when you sneeze, do not share germs!

Pinky: Yeah! Hooooray! I got it, said Pinky. "May I have my ice cream now?"

"Sure," said Phantom. "First, help me clean up these papers."

Meowmy's Return

It was the end of the school year, and it was time for summer again. Pinky raced up to Phantom, very excited and happy about something.

"Well," Phantom exclaimed, "what is it that has made you so excited this day?"

"Great news!" said Pinky. "The most wonderful news. I just saw my friend Meowmy's grandmother, and she told me Meowmy will be coming back to spend the summer here in Barrwood City. I can't wait," said Pinky. "I can't sit still. I missed my friend Meowmy, and now she will be back to visit."

Meowmy was due to arrive the next day, and Pinky could not wait. He was even too excited to sleep. He tried everything to go to sleep, counting sheep, warm milk, and lullaby songs, but nothing worked. Instead, Pinky stayed up and thought about all the games that he will play with Meowmy until he fell asleep.

The next day, early in the morning, Pinky woke up to the slamming of a car door. Then he heard a familiar voice. It was Meowmy! Pinky leapt up out of bed, dragged on his clothes, and started to race out the door.

"Not so fast, Pinky," said Phantom. "You still have to brush your teeth and wash your face."

Pinky knew it was important do those every morning, so he quickly race to the bathroom to wash his face and brush his teeth. Then off he went to meet his friend, Meowmy.

He raced down the stairs, out the front door, and to the house across

Meowmy's Return

the street where Meowmy was staying. Pinky stopped as he was about to cross the street; he knew it was important to stop and look both ways before crossing the street. Luckily, he stopped just in time because a car zoomed right pass him and would have hit him if he had not stopped. When it was clear, Pinky ran across the street, and there stood Meowmy, waiting for him.

"Oh, Pinky my friend," said Meowmy. "I missed you so much and couldn't wait to come back and play with you."

"I also missed you," said Pinky, "and looked forward to playing our games again."

The two friends hugged each other and wanted to play immediately. "Bye, Grammy. Pinky and I are going to play now," said Meowmy, and off they went.

Meowmy's Return

The two friends played for hours; only stopping for lunch. They played after lunch and close to dinner time. Then the sun started to set. Finally, Phantom had to call them as it started to get late.

"Pinnnkky! Meowwwmmy! It is getting late, it is time to go in, wash up and have dinner."

"Can we just play a little bit longer?" asked Pinky.

"I am afraid not it will be dark soon," said Phantom. "Besides, you should save some games for later. You both have the rest of the summer to play. Don't wear yourselves out in one day. You will not have the energy to play on other days."

"Okay. I guess you are right," agreed the two friends.

All three cats went home, singing the friendship song they made up:

Meowmy's Return

We are happy, as happy as can be

I got you and friend you've got me

We will share and care and play all the day

And when you're sad I will only have happy things to say

Cause we're friends no matter what comes what may

A friend is what I'll be and a friend is what I'll stay

I L.O.V.E. Y.O.U., my friend

I L.O.V.E. Y.O.U. my friend

I L.O.V.E. Y.O.U., myyyy frieeeend

                    The End

Phantom and Pinky's Day In

"I'm bored," exclaimed Pinky, as he looked out at the rain coming down. "Well, we can't go outside," said Phantom, and then asked Pinky what he would like to do.

Pinky wanted to play. It has been raining all morning, and he was tired of being in the house. Phantom told him that there were lots of fun things to do in the house, but Pinky just shook his head in disbelief. Phantom saw at the sad look on Pinky's face and right away he had an idea. He raced off, leaving Pinky to stare out at the rain from the bedroom window.

Phantom rushed down to the basement to look for some of their old Halloween costumes. "Aha," he said, "I found them." In his paws were two pirate costumes they wore two years back. He thought, "We can play pirates' treasure hunt." Since they could not play outside, Phantom thought this would be a great indoor game to play.

He then started on the plans for the game. First, he drew a treasure map, but that was not your ordinary treasure map. Instead of an X-marks-the-spot treasure map, he drew a treasure map with many X marks to mark the spots. Each X would provide a clue leading to the next X until the final X is reached where a bounty of treasures would be found.

In their case, the treasure was an old box filled with chocolate wrapped in gold wrapping paper and made to look like gold coins. Pinky is going to have so much fun, Phantom thought.

"Pinky, we are going to have some fun here inside the house," said Phantom. "We are going to play pirates."

Phantom jumped into the room wearing his pirate costume and told Pinky to put on his costume. Pinky was so excited and raced to put on his pirate outfit. They both made paper swords and set out to have a pirate adventure. They followed the map to all corners of the house, each trip leading to a different adventure.

They battled crocodiles as they crossed Swampland Valley; they climbed the highest cliffs of Bed Mountain, and hiked up the Stairs of Doom.

Finally, they reached the end of their journey at the final X where the box of gold stood. They both stood there for a few seconds, staring at the box full shiny booty, amazed at the wonders of their treasure. Pinky had so much fun getting to the treasure that he did not want it to end.

Phantom and Pinky's Day In

When Phantom opened up one of the golden coins to reveal the hidden chocolate pieces, Pinky quickly raced over to join him. The two sat there and ate while having a laugh at the amazing adventure they had together. Pinky finally stopped laughing and said, "I wish that it rains again tomorrow."

Phantom then replied, "See, I told you we can have fun inside."

The End

The Differences We See

There was a buzz of excitement in the air. Phantom was rushing around in glee, as he prepared for the visit of his brother, Casper. He had not seen his little brother for quite some time now, and he could not contain his joy. Pinky was happy for Phantom, and as any great friend would do, he did everything he could do to help Phantom get ready for Casper's visit. They had a great big feast planned and invited everyone over to welcome Casper. Everything was beautiful.

Soon a taxi pulled up to the curve and stopped in front of Phantom and Pinky's house. It was Casper! He was strangely very different from Phantom. He was a white cat with patches of gray, and Phantom was tan with streaks of black all over his coat. The biggest difference of all was very noticeable in their eyes. Casper had two different-colored eyes, one green and one blue, and Phantom did not, but they were indeed brothers.

"Phantom, is that your brother?" asked Pinky as he looked out the front window.

"Yes, he is here," replied Phantom. Phantom hurried outside to greet Casper. "Welcome! Welcome! Welcome!" he exclaimed.

After a very long hug, the two cats went inside the house where the others were waiting. Everyone stood inside at the entrance of the house in a line to greet Casper. As Phantom introduced Casper down the line of greeters, each one welcomed Casper with a smile and a hearty handshake, some even gave him a great big hug. Finally, at the end of the line, there stood Pinky.

Phantom said, "And last but not least, this is my best friend in the whole wide world, Pinky."

Casper reached out to shake Pinky's hand, but all Pinky could do was stand there, mesmerized by Casper's eyes. He suddenly felt ashamed of himself for staring at Casper and for the way he treated him that he darted off to hide. After a few minutes of searching, Phantom found Pinky hiding in his closet by following the sound of a sobbing Pinky.

The Differences We See

"Pinky, why did you run off like that and why are you crying?" Phantom asked.

Pinky told Phantom he was ashamed of the way he reacted to Casper. He thought Casper was not normal because of the way he looked. "He is weird because he had two different color eyes," Pinky explained.

"It is true that he does look different, but that does not mean he is different from the rest of us," Phantom told Pinky. Phantom went on to tell him that not everyone in the world will be the same. "Some people will have similar traits and similar likes, but we are all different in our own way. Even though we are all different individually, overall, we are all the same as a group. Casper has two different color eyes, and I think that makes him stand out. They are one of the first things we see when we look at Casper, but we cannot use that to define him." Phantom continued to say, "We should not just focus on the differences we see in someone, but focus more on what makes them the same as us. For instance, Casper likes to play just like us. He likes to eat sweets and also likes to play computer games just like us," explained Phantom. "So you see, he is not that different from us at all."

Pinky finally calmed down, and with a look of relief on his face followed by a charming little smile, Pinky responded to Phantom, "Let's play our favorite game with Casper, treasure hunt!"

Phantom agreed and the two went back to the party. Pinky apologized to Casper and gave him a big hug to welcome him to their home.

Pinky: How do you feel about treasure hunts?
Casper: Treasure hunts? I love treasure hunts!
Pinky: Then I have a great game for us to play.
And they played happily ever after.

The End

Pinky

Phantom

Made in the USA
Middletown, DE
10 March 2023

26552281R00029